Aztec Man: The Hero

Original Story by John F. Knippel
2022
Original Artwork by Beverly A. Knippel
2022
Characters based upon the book
Ancient Mexico by Maria Longhena
1998

Announcer: G G G G O O O O A A A A L L L L

Jesus: I wish I were better at soccer. I try, but the goalie always blocks my shots. I'm such a loser.

Aztec Man: Hey there, don't be so hard on yourself.

J.S. Who are you? Where did you come from?

A.M. I'm Aztec Man. I am a time-traveler sent to help you.

J.S. Help me? Who sent you? Is this a joke? Are you my dad in disguise?

A.M. Whoa there. One question at a time. Yes, you – the Hero Twins – not a joke – I'm not your dad. Now then, are you serious about getting better at soccer?

J.S. Well, if you are real, then yes. How can you help me get better? And who are the Hero Twins anyway. Never heard of them.

A.M. Again, one question at a time. I can help by taking you to see the Hero Twins, watch them play, and learn how to score more goals.

J.S How do we get there?

A.M. Grip my hand tightly. Time travel to ancient Tenochtitlan is very fast and powerful. Here we go!

J.S. Whew! That as rough! Is this the ancient Mexico City?

A.M. Yes, it is. Over there, to your left, is the soccer stadium. Let's watch the Twins play. Then, I will introduce you to them.

J.S. Wow, they are really good! Look at that hip shot!

A.M. Their goal is not a netted cage on the ground. They must make it through the ring near the top of the wall.

J.S. Gosh, I though soccer goals were hard to make.

AFTER THE GAME

A.M. Hero Twins, this is Jesus. He needs your help.

H.T. Yes, we saw you through our epoch-scope. You have good physical skill.

J.S. Then why can't I score more goals?

H.T. The answer to that question is trickery.

J.S. What do you mean trickery?

H.T. You let the goalie and the defender both know when and how you are attempting to score.

J.S. What can I do to change that?

H.T. Set your sight on the spot you will shot

from, BUT don't stare at it. Let your mind guide

your feet. Look somewhere else with your eyes

and head moves. Trust your body and shoot

when you get to the spot.

H.T. Also, sometimes pass the ball to your team mates. That keeps the defender off balance. The keys are knowing where your team mates are and trusting your body. Remember, this is a TEAM sport, not only you against them.

J.S. Wow! That's simple. Trust my body and my friends. We're in this together.

A.M. Time's up on this trip, Jesus. Let's get back home before someone misses you.

J.S. Oh, yeah! I'm ready. Let's do this! Thanks Hero Twins and Aztec Man.

J.S. Gosh, Those pyramids and the ball court were really great to see.

Back home again, Jesus is again on the soccer field. This time results are different.

The End

ADDENDUM

1. The Capital of Ancient Mexico was Tenochtitlan

2. The "Aztec Man" is modeled after a clay statue as found in the book <u>Ancient Mexico</u> by Maria Longhena, 1998

3. The "Sacred Ball Game" (tlachtli) may have been a forerunner of today's soccer and basketball

4. The Aztec warriors wrote poetry similar to the English knights of the same period

5. The pyramids were a place of worship

Other Books by John and Bev Knippel

Peace be With You

Praise II

Homeless: Hand out or Hand Up?

M.L.C.R. Visual Search Patterns for Safe Driving

Buttercup: A Rescue Dog Story

Buttercup II
Miss Hollywood and Woofy Visit

Tales of the Aztecs

Muddy Mayans

RACCA; Don't Call a Man a Fool

Coming Soon

Aztec Woman

Praise III

Made in the USA
Columbia, SC
23 July 2022

63926694R00018